"THE FLYING SHE-DEVILS" AND "THE SPARROW" CREATED BY
BRIAN CLEVINGER *and* **SCOTT WEGENER**

IDW

Facebook: **facebook.com/idwpublishing**
Twitter: **@idwpublishing**
YouTube: **youtube.com/idwpublishing**
Tumblr: **tumblr.idwpublishing.com**
Instagram: **instagram.com/idwpublishing**

COVER ART BY
SCOTT WEGENER
AND ANTHONY CLARK

COLLECTION EDITS BY
JUSTIN EISINGER
AND ALONZO SIMON

ORIGINAL DESIGN BY
JEFF POWELL

ADDITIONAL DESIGN
ERIC TRAUTMANN /
FEDORA MONKEY STUDIO

PUBLISHER
TED ADAMS

978-1-68405-002-4   21 20 19 18   1 2 3 4

REAL SCIENCE ADVENTURES: THE FLYING SHE-DEVILS IN RAID ON MARAUDER ISLAND. JANUARY 2018. FIRST PRINTING.

ATOMIC ROBO PRESENTS REAL SCIENCE ADVENTURES

THE FLYING SHE-DEVILS IN RAID ON MARAUDER ISLAND

WORDS
BRIAN CLEVINGER

ART
LO BAKER

COLORS
ANTHONY CLARK

LETTERS
TESSA STONE

THE SPARROW IN PROJECT MILLIPEDE

WORDS
BRIAN CLEVINGER

ART
WOOK JIN CLARK

COLORS
ANTHONY CLARK

LETTERS
JEFF POWELL

EDITS
LEE BLACK

INTRODUCTION

WOMEN HAVE BEEN A VITAL PART OF AVIATION AND AEROSPACE since the very beginning. *She-Devils* captures the essence of bravery, sacrifice, and determination of women in the post World War II era. Empowered by the roles they took up to support the war effort, they became engineers, pilots, and aircraft assembly technicians. When the war ended, and many were told to "get back to the kitchen," many American women instead pushed for the stars. With trailblazers such as Bessie Coleman and Harriet Quimby as role models, Amelia Earhart, Jackie Cochran, and dozens of other women defied stereotypes and forged the future of Aviation and Aerospace in this country and around the world.

As a commercial pilot and flight instructor myself, I take great pride in, and draw inspiration everyday from this long line of courageous women aviators. As a female professional working in the aviation industry for over 20 years, I am humbled to see how far we have come. I am encouraged by the efforts of organizations like Women in Aviation International, The Ninety-Nines, Inc., and the Experimental Aircraft Association, as well as many others, to inspire young women to get involved in careers in Aviation and Aerospace, to see their true potential, to cast off preconceived notions of their limitations, and rise... rise... *rise* above. Above the clouds, and above the stars, the future awaits us, and a woman will surely be one of humanity's guides!

Julie Seltsam-Wilps
FAASTeam Services Provider
FAA Aviation Education Program Manager
Pilot / Operations
Merrimack, NH

ART BY SCOTT WEGENER
COLORS BY ANTHONY CLARK

GIVE 'EM HELL

1

SOUTH PACIFIC, 1946
CLEAR THE CAVE. WE'RE COMING IN.
ROGER.

SHE-DEVIL ISLAND

CAP WON'T BE HAPPY.
NO.

READY?
YOU SURE THIS WON'T BLOW UP?
PRETTY SURE.
LAUREN. YOU SAID THAT LAST TIME.
SURE, CAP. BUT I WAS LYING THAT TIME.
WELL. THAT JUST GIVES ME ALL KINDS OF CONFIDENCE.
WHAT'S THIS?
PROTECTION.
USUALLY I ADMIRE YOUR OPTIMISM.
YOU WORRY TOO MUCH, CAP.
AND I HOPE TO FOR A LONG TIME.

CLK!
GLK
CLK
CLK
CLK
CLK
CLK
VRRR-
VWOOOSH
PFEHHH

IT WORKED!

BARELY.
BARELY WORKING IS THE FIRST STEP TO WORKING GREAT ALL THE TIME.

AND WE'RE SUPPOSED TO WEAR THESE? ON OUR BACKS?
THEY'LL LET US FLY CIRCLES AROUND ANYTHING WITH WINGS!

AT LEAST, THE NEXT MODEL WILL.
WILL THAT ONE BE ANY SAFER?
WORKING ON IT.

CAP. GOT A MINUTE?

THE HAUL WAS THAT BAD?
HOW'D YOU GUESS?
YOUR FACE SAYS IT ALL.
REALLY? THOUGHT I WAS HIDING IT PRETTY GOOD.
UH. DON'T PLAY POKER, HAZEL.

THAT'S THE SECOND SUPPLY RUN IN A ROW WE CAME UP EMPTY-HANDED.
WE CAN'T KEEP THIS GOING IF THERE'S NOTHING TO SCAVENGE.
YOU KNOW WHAT I SUGGEST.
WE'RE JUST STARTING TO GET SETTLED HERE. WE CAN'T PACK UP AND MOVE. NOT AGAIN. WE NEED A HOME.

I'M NOT SAYING I WANT TO.
BUT WANT TO DO AND GOT TO DO ARE TWO DIFFERENT THINGS.

IT'S SAFE HERE.
YEAH, BECAUSE THE ISLAND'S UNCHARTED.
OFFICE

OFFICE
AND, OKAY, THAT KEEPS US SAFE FROM RAIDERS. BUT IT'S ALSO WHY OUR SUPPLY RUNS ARE COMING UP SHORT. THERE'S NOTHING LEFT IN RANGE!

I THINK CAPTAIN IS RIGHT.

THANK YOU, VALERYA.

THIS IS HOME. WE NOT RUNNING.

LOOK.
I LIKE IT HERE *TOO.* HELL, WE *ALL* DO.

BUT IF WE DON'T FIND A WAY TO EXPAND OUR RANGE, AND I MEAN *SOON,* THEN ALL WE CAN DO IS PACK UP AND HEAD OUT.
WE'VE GOT, *MAYBE,* TWO WEEKS OF FOOD AND WATER.

THE LONGER WE STAY, THE WORSE OUR CHANCES GET. IF WE'RE GONNA GO, WE GOTTA DO IT *NOW.*

LAUREN'S ON THE VERGE OF A BREAKTHROUGH WITH THOSE ROCKETS.
GREAT. BUT THEY'LL HAVE SHORTER RANGE THAN THE PLANES. THEY DON'T FIX THIS PROBLEM.

IT'LL SET HER BACK MONTHS TO SHUT DOWN NOW.
THAT'S STILL BETTER THAN STARVING TO DEATH.
THERE IS ONE TARGET. VERY VIABLE.
MAD JACK'S MARAUDERS.
THERE ANYONE ON THIS ISLAND WITH A LICK OF SENSE?
MAYBE "VIABLE" MEANS SOMETHING ELSE IN RUSSIAN.
MAD JACK'S THE CLOSEST THING TO A KING OUT HERE.
WE DON'T HAVE HALF THE NUMBERS TO PULL OFF WHATEVER YOU'RE THINKING.
YOU DON'T KNOW WHAT I THINKING.
I REALLY DON'T.
WE GO TO THEM. NIGHT RAID. LIKE IN THE WAR.
WE DITCH PLANES.
WE TAKE THEIR SUNDERLAND.

MAD JACK'S FLAGSHIP? THE HARBINGER OF DREAD?
IS FLYING BOAT. CAN GO ANYWHERE. CARRY ANYTHING.
HOME AWAY FROM HOME.
WE STAY. AND EXPAND RANGE.
HOW MANY DO YOU NEED TO FLY A SUNDERLAND?
FIVE. MAYBE FOUR.
REALLY? MY IDEA WAS CRAZY, BUT THE SUICIDE MISSION ISN'T?
IT'S NOT SUICIDE.
OH? MAD JACK'S JUST GONNA LET US HAVE THE PRIZE OF HIS FLEET?
OF COURSE NOT, BUT THINK ABOUT IT.
NOTHING IN THE PACIFIC FLIES AS FAR AS A SUNDERLAND.
ALL WE HAVE TO DO IS STAY ALIVE LONGER THAN THEY CAN STAY AIRBORNE.

EASIER SAID THAN DONE.

SABOTAGE AIRFIELD. EVERY SECOND COUNTS.
BRING ALL STICKY BOMB WE CAN CARRY.

I STILL DON'T LIKE IT. TOO MANY VARIABLES AND ALL OF THEM ARE OUT OF OUR CONTROL.
WHAT IF SOMETHING GOES WRONG?

THEN WE'RE DEAD. THERE'S NO MAKING IT HALFWAY ON THIS ONE.
SO, LIKE I SAID. SUICIDE MISSION.

ONLY IF WE DIE.

OKAY. FINE. WHO'S GOING?
VOLUNTEERS. FOUR GIRLS.

IS MY IDEA. I VOLUNTEERS.
COUNT ME IN TOO.

I'LL VOLUNTEER SO SOMEONE ELSE DOESN'T HAVE TO.

NO. NOT BOTH OF US.
IF IT IS A SUICIDE MISSION, SOMEONE NEEDS TO FIND OUR GIRLS A NEW HOME.

THERE'S NO ONE ELSE I'D TRUST TO RUN THIS OUTFIT.

GOSH.

DO I GET YOUR CAPTAIN'S HAT?

I'M LEADING THE CHARGE. VAL'S MY SECOND.
WE JUST NEED TWO MORE. ANY VOLUNTEERS?

NOT SURE WHAT I EXPECTED.
LIZ, SARA. YOU'RE ON DECK.

THE REST OF YOU, YOU'VE GOT SOME PLANES TO PREP.

I'M TIRED OF RUNNING, VAL.
I CAN'T ASK THESE GIRLS TO PACK UP. NOT AGAIN.

WORRIER TOO MUCH.
I HAVE TO. I'M RESPONSIBLE FOR WHAT HAPPENS TO US. YOU'RE ALL OUT HERE BECAUSE OF ME.

NO.
WE ***CHOOSE*** BEING HERE. NO ONE DID THAT FOR US.

THESE ARE STRONG GIRLS. CAPABLE.
OF COURSE THEY ARE. BUT WE'VE NEVER DONE ANYTHING AS DANGEROUS AS THIS JOB.

COULD RAID PETE'S. AGAIN.

WON'T LIE, I BEEN THINKING ABOUT IT. BUT NO.
ONCE WAS MAKING A POINT. *TWICE* IS ASKING FOR PAYBACK.

THIS MISSION. WHAT IS *WORST* CAN HAPPEN?
UH, WE *DIE.*

AND IF WE *NOT* DO THIS? WHAT IS WORST THEN?
WE DIE *ANYWAY.*
OKAY. THEN NOTHING TO WORRY ABOUT.

I CAN'T *BELIEVE* THAT'S REASSURING.

CAP. WE'RE READY.

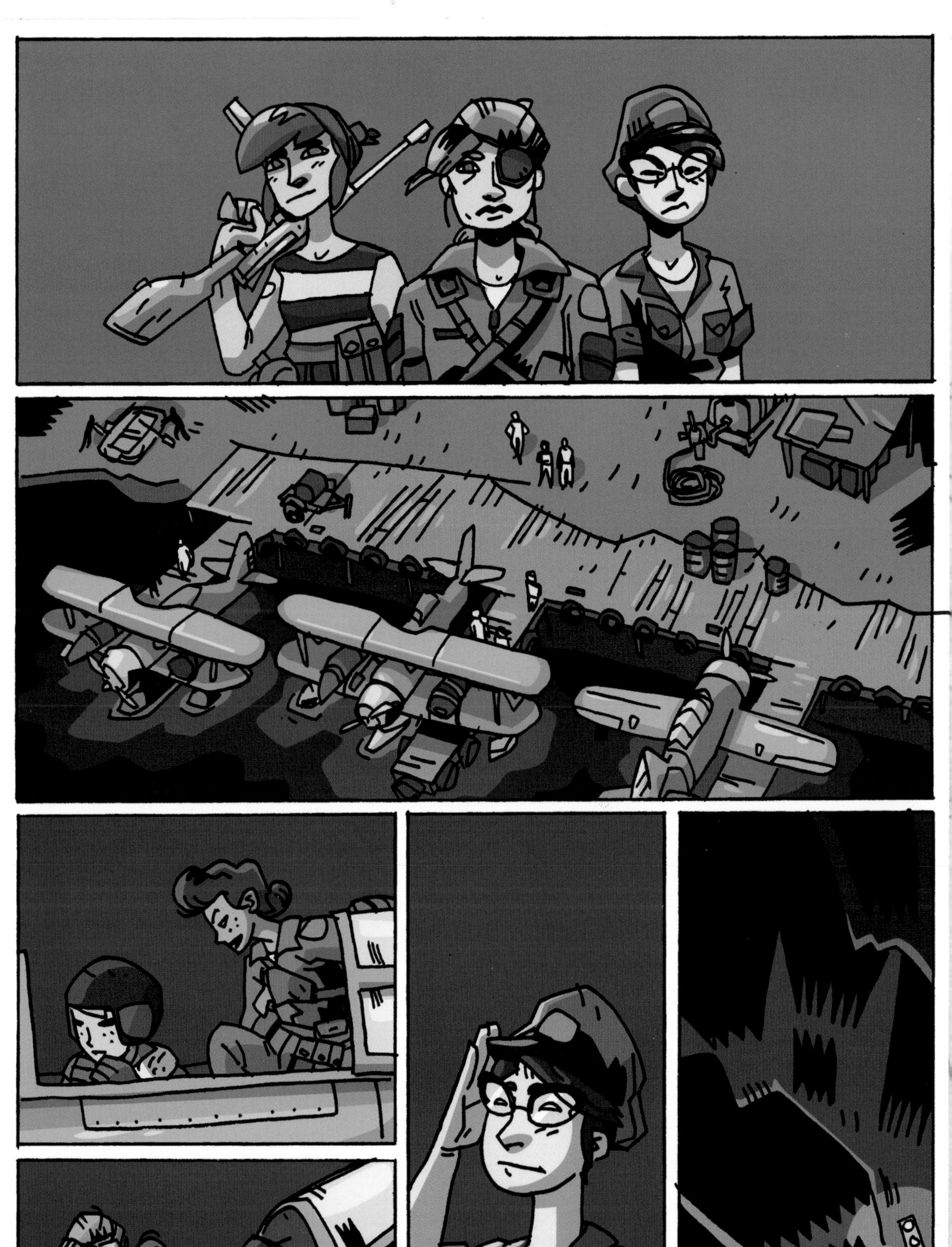

BWARRRRRR

GIVE 'EM HELL.

ART BY SCOTT WEGENER
COLORS BY ANTHONY CLARK

WE STRIKE AT NIGHT

2

GETTING THE BOAT UP TOOK ABOUT AN HOUR LONGER THAN WE FIGURED.
STILL. WE SHOULD MAKE LAND BY NIGHTFALL WITH PLENTY OF DARK TO SPARE.
MARAUDER ISLAND

YOU SMELL THAT?
IS BOOZE?
THEN IT'S *BAD* HOOCH. MAYBE *GASOLINE?*

IT'S PIRATES.

THEY LOOK DEAD.
OR LIKE THEY'LL WAKE UP WISHIN' THEY *WERE*.

KEEP FOCUSED. THEIR AIRFIELD CAN'T BE TOO FAR NOW.

JACKPOT!
NO. HARBINGER IS JACKPOT.
DON'T SEE HER NOWHERE.
SHE'D BE IN THE WATER.

THERE.

LIZ, SARA. SABOTAGE.
VAL. YOU'RE WITH ME.
KEEP OUT OF SIGHT OF THE HUTS.

MAKE SURE SHE'S TOPPED OFF. I'LL START THE PREFLIGHT.

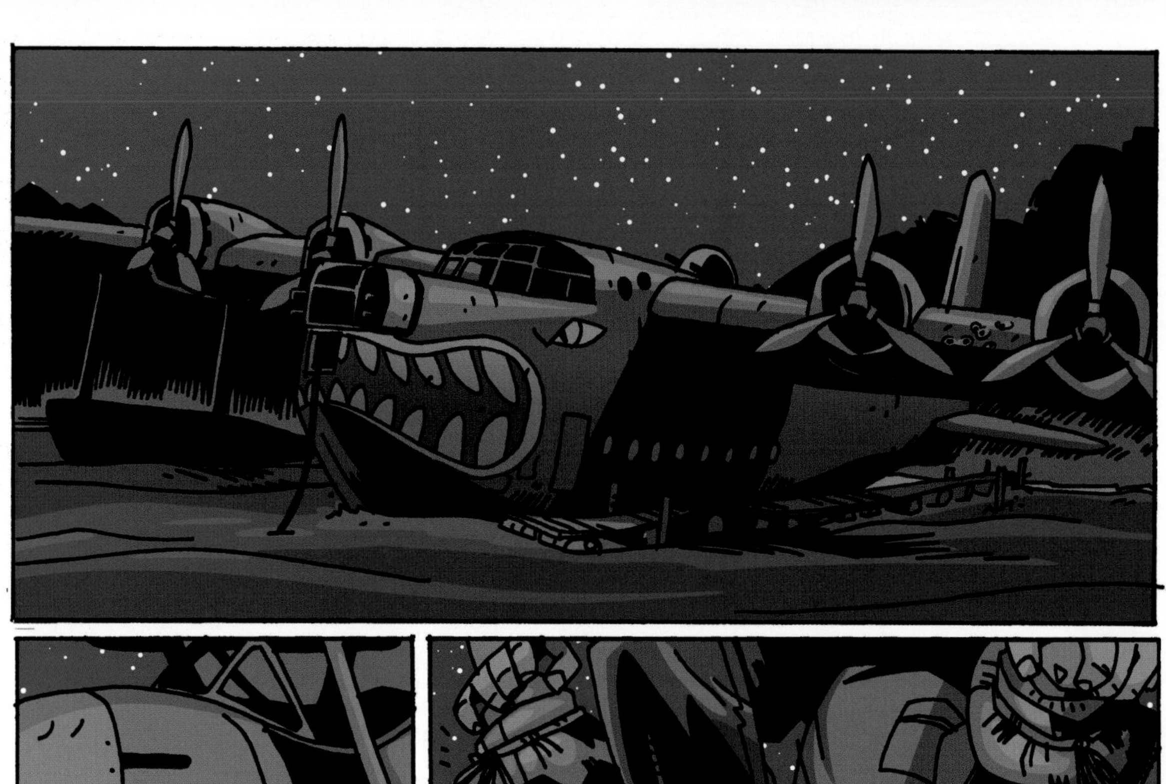

SNF
SNF

TSK

GIRL, QUIT HUFFING GAS FUMES AND GET TO WORK!

I'M NOT HUFFING ANYTHING! AND I DON'T THINK THEY KEEP GAS IN HERE.
YEAH, I MEAN, ANYTHING COULD BE IN FUEL DRUMS NEXT TO AIRPLANES.

HOW MANY FUEL DRUMS GOT LADLES?
OKAY, *THAT'S* WEIRD.

COUGH!

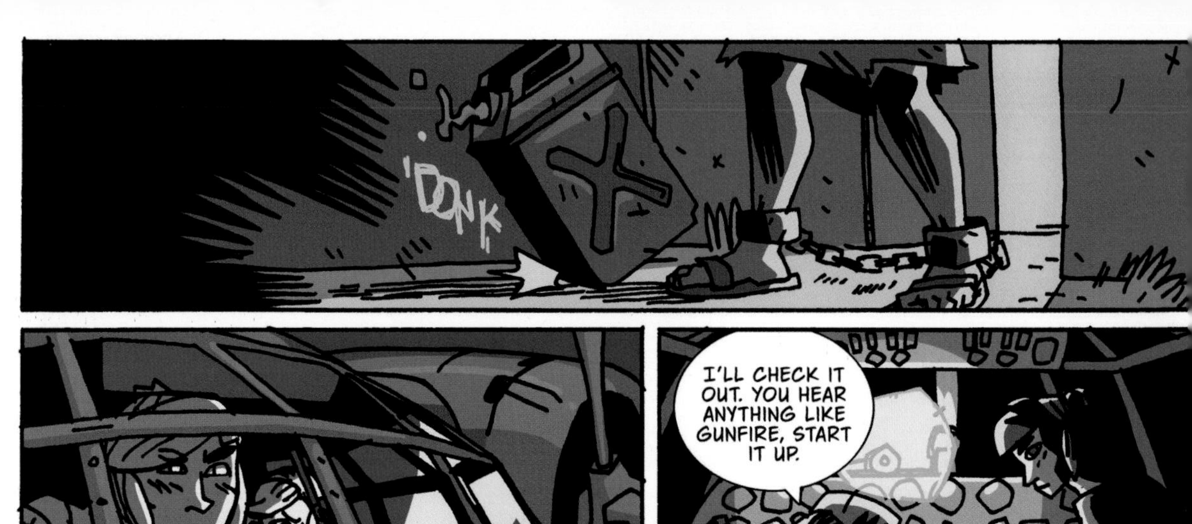
'DONK

HEAR THAT?

I'LL CHECK IT OUT. YOU HEAR ANYTHING LIKE GUNFIRE, START IT UP.

DAMN THOSE GIRLS.

WHO ARE THEY?
ISLANDERS. FROM TONGA.
WE THINK.
THEY SOUND TONGAN.

WE THINK THEY'RE MAKIN' FUEL. SMELLS LIKE TORPEDO JUICE.
OR SOME KINDA HIGH-OCTANE OKOLEHAO.
WE GOTTA TAKE 'EM WITH US, CAP.
NOT A CHANCE. WE CAN'T PUT THEM IN THAT KIND OF DANGER.

YOU THINK IT'S SAFER TO LEAVE 'EM HERE?

WHO ARE THEY?! WHERE OUR GIRLS?
I'LL EXPLAIN IN THE AIR. START THE PLANE.

IT WOULD BE SHAME TO KEEP PLAN SIMPLE.

DID WE TAG ALL THEIR PLANES?
IT'S ALL THE BOMBS WE GOT EITHER WAY.
WE COULD GRAB SOME FROM THE STILLS?
PFOOOOM!
THIS IS WHY YOU'RE STARTING THE PLANE.
THAT MIGHTA WOKE 'EM UP.

THE HOOCH!

WHUZZAT?

FIRE! FIRE IN THE HOOCH!
BUCKET TEAMS! NOW!

AND I'M KILLIN' THE LAST MAN T'GET HIS FEET UNDER 'IM!

PROTECT THE HOOCH!

BOSS! LOOK!

SHE-DEVILS.
TAKE THE FLYBOYS AND GET THE HARBINGER BACK.

THE REST OF YOU GET THAT FIRE UNDER CONTROL!

FA
BOOM

WE'RE GOOD TO GO, CAP!
KCHNK

EVERYONE STRAPPED DOWN?
ABOUT AS GOOD AS THEY'RE GONNA BE.

BWARRF

THAT WAS THE LAST OF THE GAS!
NO IT *WEREN'T.* THERE'S WHAT'S LEFT IN OUR WARBIRDS.

BFOOM
POOM

KRA-BOOM

GET TO THE SEAPLANES.

NOT YOU.

BLAM

SAID I'D KILL THE LAST MAN T'GET UP.

WELL. IF WE'RE LUCKY, THEN THE HARD PART'S OVER.
THAT WAS TOO EASY TO BE THE HARD PART.
THERE'S THAT FAMOUS RUSSIAN OPTIMISM.
HRM.
YOU GONNA BE SALTY AT ME UNTIL I EXPLAIN ABOUT OUR PASSENGERS?
YES.

LIZ AND SARA FOUND 'EM CHAINED UP AND MAKIN' SOME KINDA GASOLINE MOONSHINE FOR THE MARAUDERS.
HELL, THEY'RE PROBABLY HOW MAD JACK CAME TO RULE THESE SEAS.
YES. HE WILL NOT LET THEM GO WITHOUT FIGHT.

WE ALREADY HAD A FIGHT ON OUR HANDS. AT LEAST NOW IT'S FOR SOMETHING MORE THAN A PLANE.
THAT IS THE TROUBLE. THEY CAN LIVE WITHOUT THE PLANE.

GONNA NEED ONE OF YOU ON THE TAIL GUN ASAP.

LOVE TO OBLIGE, CAP. BUT WE'RE STILL GETTIN' NAV AND ENGINEERING UP TO SPEED SO WE DON'T, Y'KNOW, *CRASH.*

THERE'S SOME TIME. BUT MAKE IT QUICK ALL THE SAME.
WE CAN'T RISK MAD JACK GETTING THE DROP ON US.

THINK THEY CAN SHOOT?

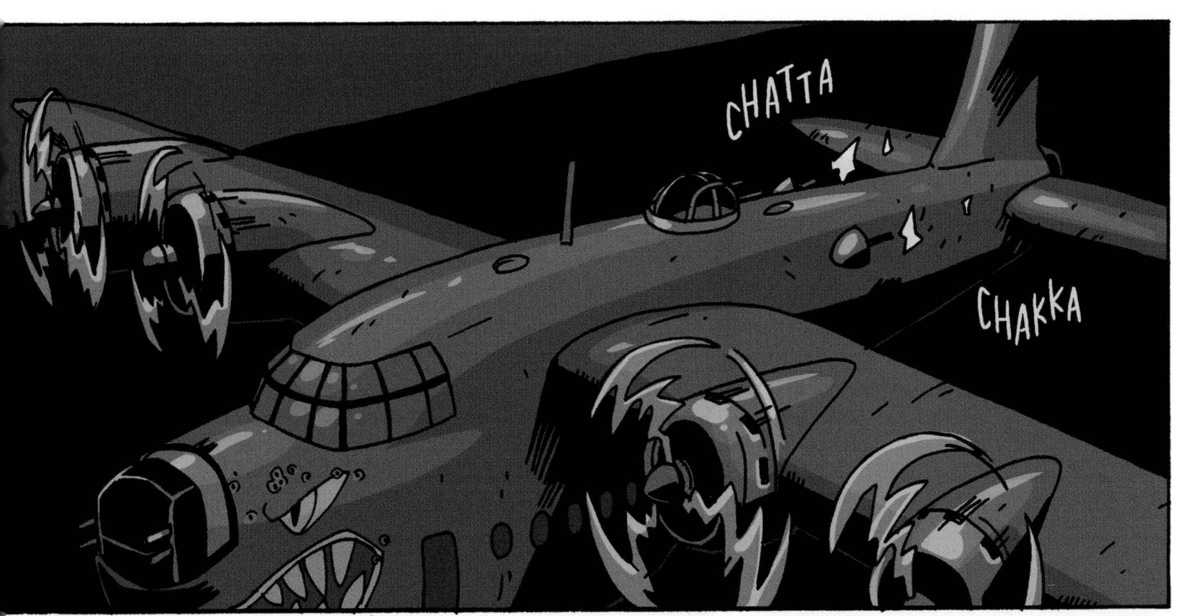
CHATTA
CHAKKA

NOT CHATTA, CHATTA, CHATTA, CHATTA.
JUST CHATTA. GOT IT?

OKAY. LET'S SHOW 'EM HOW TO WORK THE TURRETS.

I GOT 'EM!
I GOT 'EM!
GOOD! KEEP OUTTA SIGHT UNTIL WE GET THERE.

MARAUDERS! CHECK YOUR GUNS AND READY FOR BOARDING.

ART BY SCOTT WEGENER
COLORS BY ANTHONY CLARK

SKY RAIDERS OF THE PACIFIC

3

30, 000 FT OVER THE PACIFIC OCEAN

HOW WE DOIN', GIRLS?

ON COURSE AND AHEAD OF SCHEDULE, CAP.

WE WON'T FALL OUTTA THE SKY. FOR A WHILE ANYWAY.
BUT WE'RE USIN' MORE GAS THAN WE FIGURED.

GOOD!
VERY GOOD!

THEY PICK UP ENGLISH FAST.

HOPE THEY LEARN TO SHOOT EVEN FASTER.

LIZ. WHAT'S BURNING UP OUR GO-JUICE?
COULDN'T SAY, CAP. CAN'T BE THE WEIGHT, WE'RE PRACTICALLY EMPTY.

GAS NOT PURE. MIXED WITH HIGH OCTANE HOOCH. TONGANS MAKE IT.
STRETCHES FUEL, BUT LESS EFFICIENT. WE NEED CHANGE OF PLAN.
TONGA HOOCH MADE MAD JACK KING. WON'T STOPPING UNTIL HE GETS THEM BACK.

OR HE DIES TRYING.
YES. WE SHOULD HIDE UNTIL THAT HAPPENS.

WE CAN'T LAY LOW.
OUR GIRLS ARE WAITING FOR US. IF WE DON'T MAKE IT TO THE RENDEZVOUS POINT IN TIME, THEY'LL HAVE NO CHOICE BUT TO PULL BACK.
AND IF WE MISS THEM, WE'LL BE STUCK IN THE MIDDLE OF THE OCEAN WITH NO FUEL, NO FOOD, AND NO WAY HOME.

THERE'S NO SAFE WAY THROUGH THIS. BEST WE CAN DO IS TAKE OUR CHANCES WITH MAD JACK.

Y'NEVER KNOW. THEY MIGHT NOT CATCH UP TO US IN THE FIRST PLACE.
CAP? I JUST RAN THE NEW NUMBERS ON OUR GAS FROM LIZ.

WE'RE GONNA HAVE A HARD TIME MAKING IT TO THE RENDEZVOUS AS IS.

DAMMIT.
OKAY, GONNA SEE WHAT I CAN DO WITH THESE ENGINES TO GET **EVERY LAST MILE** OUT OF 'EM.

HOW CLOSE **CAN** WE GET?

AS OF OUR CURRENT COURSE AND SPEED?
UH. CLOSE-**ISH.**
CLOSE ENOUGH THEY COULD **SPOT** US IN THE AIR?
IF IT'S BRIGHT AND CLEAR. **MAYBE?**

AS LONG AS THEY **SEE** US, IT'S CLOSE **ENOUGH.**
WILLING TO GAMBLE **LIVES** ON IT?

I CAN SEE TO IT WE GET **THAT** CLOSE, CAP.
BUT WE **GOTTA** TAKE IT EASY. ANY BIG MANEUVERS'LL BURN MORE FUEL THAN I CAN **SAVE.**

PIRATE, PIRATE!

WHAT BEARING?
TONGAN DON'T KNOW CLOCKS.
HADN'T THOUGHT OF THAT.

SHE-DEVILS!
YOU STOLE MY PLANE AND MY WOMEN.
YOUR BOLDNESS HAS EARNED YOU A CHOICE. RETURN THEM OR DIE WITH THEM.

BLUFFING. HE MIGHT RISK THE PLANE. NEVER THE TONGANS.

MAD JACK.
YOU'RE MISTAKEN. THIS AIN'T YOUR PLANE. THESE AIN'T YOUR WOMEN. LEAVE US BE. THERE'S NOTHING HERE FOR YOU BUT DEATH.

WHAT A DISAPPOINTMENT.
WHEN YOU ARE DROWNING IN BLOOD AND FLAMES AND SEA, I WANT YOU TO REMEMBER IT WAS YOUR CHOICE.

WARBIRDS! ADVANCE!

FUEL
MAIN TANK
UH, CAP?

WE CAN'T OUTRUN 'EM, WE CAN'T OUTFLY 'EM, AND WE CAN'T OUTGUN 'EM.

ALL WE GOTTA DO IS OUTLAST 'EM.

TATATAT
TAK
TAK
TAK

CHAKA

TAK
TAK

NOTHING TO CHEER UNTIL THEY SHOT DOWN.

WHY'RE THEY ONLY ***PLAYIN'*** WITH US? WE'RE SITTIN' DUCKS UNTIL THOSE GIRLS LEARN TO ***SHOOT.***

SIMPLE. MAD JACK WANTS PLANE ***AND*** PRISONERS ***WITHOUT*** HOLES.
YEAH. MAYBE.
WHAT ELSE?

DISTRACTION.

PIRATE, PIRATE!

PIRATE!

WHY AIN'T YA *SHOOTIN'* THEM?

PIRATES!

SON OF A-!

BOSS! YOU WAS RIGHT! THEY BLIND AS BATS TOPSIDE.
FOOLS DIDN'T BRING A FULL CREW.
KEEP A LOOKOUT. MOVE IN IF OUR BOYS NEED IT.
ROGER THAT.
WHALERS! MOVE ON 'EM TOPSIDE.

BANG
BANG
BANG

NOW, CAP!

CHAKKA
CHAKKA

KCHNKA
SPT
SPFEHH

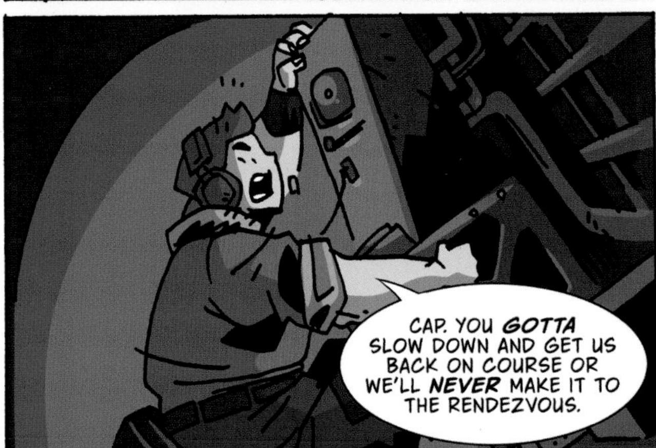
CAP. YOU **GOTTA** SLOW DOWN AND GET US BACK ON COURSE OR WE'LL **NEVER** MAKE IT TO THE RENDEZVOUS.

WON'T MAKE IT WITH THEM CLIMBING ALL OVER US NEITHER.

COURSE CORRECTION COMIN' AT YOU ***ASAP.***

WE'RE IN POSITION, BOSS!

CLEVER.
YEAH.
DID NOT EXPECT MAD JACK TO BE *CLEVER.*
ME NEITHER.

QUESTION IS, DO THEY GET *MORE* CLEVER AS THEY GET MORE *DESPERATE?*
THEY'RE RUNNING ON THE *SAME* HIGH-OCTANE BOOZE *WE* ARE. AND THEY *KNOW* WE GOT *WAY* MORE THAN *THEY* DO.

THE *LONGER* THIS GOES, THE *CRAZIER* THEY'RE GONNA GET.
WHAT IS MORE CRAZIER THAN *GRAPPLING HOOKS?*
CAP. WE MIGHT GOT A PROBLEM.

WELL, *ANOTHER* PROBLEM. PETE'S IS GONNA BE A SPELL NORTH OF OUR COURSE.
THAT'S NOTHIN' TO *US,* BUT IF *MAD JACK* FIGURES OUT HE'S JUST A *DETOUR* AWAY FROM GASSING UP...

THEN THEY'LL *OVERTAKE* US JUST AS WE'RE RUNNING ON *FUMES.*

STARTIN' TO THINK THIS TERRIBLE PLAN WAS A BAD IDEA.

WE GOT ONE CHANCE AS I SEE IT.
IF THEY GOTTA TURN AROUND TO GET TO PETE'S, THEN THAT SHOULD KEEP US AHEAD OF THEM TO THE END.

WE GOTTA BE OUR OWN BAIT.
IS TRICKY.
SARA. HOW LONG WE GOTTA KEEP THEM ON THE HOOK?

CURRENT COURSE AND SPEED? ABOUT AN HOUR.
LONGER THAN I'D LIKE. LEMME WORK UP SOME ALTERNATES.

NO. ANY DEVIATION MIGHT GET THEM THINKING TOO FAR AHEAD.
AND, JUST TO SAVE LIZ THE BREATH, WE CAN'T SPARE THE FUEL FOR A COURSE CHANGE ANYWAY.

THANKS, CAP.
AN HOUR AIN'T SO BAD AS IT SOUNDS. MAD JACK WANTS HIS PLANE AND HIS PRISONERS IN ONE PIECE, RIGHT?

SO HE'S GONNA STICK TO SCARIN' US OUT OF THE SKY FOR A WHILE YET.
OPEN FIRE SOON AS WE'RE LEVEL!

BOSS!
WE GOT GUNS ENOUGH TO KILL 'EM ALL. WHY WE KEEPIN' BACK?
WHAT GOOD'S A FLAGSHIP AT THE BOTTOM OF THE SEA? HOW MUCH GUZZLE GAS THEM TONGANS GONNA MAKE US IF THEY'RE DEAD?
DON'T STRAIN YOURSELF WITH STRATEGY. YOU BOYS ARE WEAPONS.
WEAPONS DON'T THINK. THEY ACT.
I GOT YOU HOLSTERED RIGHT NOW. BUT YOU DON'T WANT THAT. IT'S AGAINST YOUR NATURE TO BE HOLSTERED.

BUT YOU GOTTA WAIT. IT AIN'T YOUR TIME. NOT YET. BUT SOON ENOUGH.
OUR WHALERS WILL SET UPON THEM AND THEN YOU GO TO WORK.

SPEAR 'EM!

ART BY SCOTT WEGENER
COLORS BY ANTHONY CLARK

IMPROVISE OR DIE

4

THE PLANE AND THE TONGANS ARE TOO VALUABLE TO MAD JACK.

ALL WE GOTTA DO IS DRAW THEM OUT.

THEY WON'T MAKE IT EASY.

BUT AIN'T *NOTHIN'* EASY OUT HERE ANYHOW.
THREE O'CLOCK. GOT IT?

SO HOLD TIGHT. WE CAN TAKE *ANYTHING* THEY THROW AT US.

SHRANK

I GOT 'EM
I GOT 'EM!

THE HELL HIT US!
LIKE TRYIN' TO FLY A BOAT THROUGH BUTTER.

UH. CAP?

CAP, WE GOT *TROUBLE* BACK THERE.
TROUBLE UP HERE!

WHAT'S GOIN' ON?

BLEHHH!

NOPE.

LOSING SPEED.
I KNOW.
NEED MORE SPEED.
I KNOW!

WHALERS ARE DRAGGING THEM DOWN.
SWARMERS! MOVE IN.

DON'T KILL 'EM, BUT KEEP 'EM HURTING.

GRINKA
GRINKA
GRINKA

HOW YOU DOIN', LIZ?

I'M DOIN' FINE.
NOT SURE ABOUT THESE GUYS.

?!

AAUUGH!

THUNK

DID THEY LAND ON US?
GOTTA CUT THESE LINES!

LOSING SPEED.
I KNOW, VAL! WE'RE DROPPIN' LIKE A ROCK WITH WINGS.

CHANG
IT'S THE HARPOONS, CAP! WE'RE GETTIN' 'EM!

CHAKKA
CHAKKA

PIRATE, PIRATE!
SIX O'CLOCK!
CHATTA CHAT

NINE O'CLOCK!

SKROKk

GOT IT!

GAINING SPEED.
CONTROLS'RE SLUGGISH, BUT SHE'S WAKIN' UP AGAIN.
SARA. LIZ. WHERE WE GOIN' AND HOW WE DOIN'?

CHECKIN' POSITION.
DOIN' THE MATH.

CAP'N JACK, SIR!
WHICH WE'M DOWN TO NAUGHT BUT GUZZLE GAS, IF YOU PLEASE.

AND WHAT THERE IS OF *THAT*, SIR, WON'T TAKE US FAR WITH THIS MANY PLANES NEEDIN' IT.

MARAUDERS!
NO SENSE TELLIN' YOU ANYTHING BUT HOW IT IS. TANKER SAYS WE'RE LOW ON GUZZLE GAS. BUT MAD JACK'S GOT A PLAN.

WE *DIVERT.* PETE'S AIN'T MUCH OF A STRETCH FROM HERE.
BUT IT'S TOO MUCH FOR *SOME* OF YA.

SHE-DEVILS!
WAY I FIGURE IT, YOU'RE BETTIN' I WANT MY PLANE BACK. AND YOU'RE HOPIN' I KEEP WANTIN' LONG ENOUGH TO OUTLAST US.
HELL, THAT'S GOT TO BE YOUR PLAN, 'CAUSE IT'S THE ONLY CHANCE YOU GOT.

BUT SOME OF MY BOYS, THEY'RE LOW ENOUGH NOW THEY WON'T MAKE IT BACK NO HOW. I'M SENDIN' THEM YOUR WAY.
WHATEVER HAPPENS TO YOU AND TO THAT PLANE, IT'S ON YOU NOW. CAN'T NO ONE SAY WE DONE YOU WRONG.

PIRATE! TWELVE O'CLOCK! TEN O'CLOCK, EIGHT, FOUR AND EVERY O'CLOCKS!

TAKKA
TAKKA
TAKKA
POK
PAK

SKRONCH

ARE THEY RAMMING US?!

WHERE YOU GOIN'?
WE NEED MORE GUNS.
I NEED YOU HERE!
IMPROVISE.

VAL! WHAT WAS THAT?
THEY RAMMING. GUNS NOW.
I GOTTA NAVIGATE AND LIZ HAS TO GET OUR FUEL UNDER CONTROL.
SHOOT PLANES. THEN WORRY.

NOT A LOT OF GUN LEFT HERE, VAL.
IMPROVISE.

WHAT? C'MON!
YOU. NOSE GUN.

"IMPROVISE." PFAH.

JACKPOT.

PAK
POK
TAK
LOOKS LIKE I AIN'T THE ONLY ONE IMPROVISIN'.
ONLY SOME OF MAD JACK'S BOYS ARE ATTACKIN' US. THE REST ARE BREAKIN' OFF!
CHOOM
BRATATATA

PETE'S.
THEY'RE HEADIN' TO *PETE'S!*

AND KILLING *US* WITH ONES CAN'T GO THAT FAR.
OR JUST WEARIN' US OUT. EITHER WAY BENEFITS 'EM.

CHKKA
CHKKA
CHKKA

TWELVE O'CLOCK, TWELVE O'CLOCK!
CHAKK
CHAKKA

C'MON!

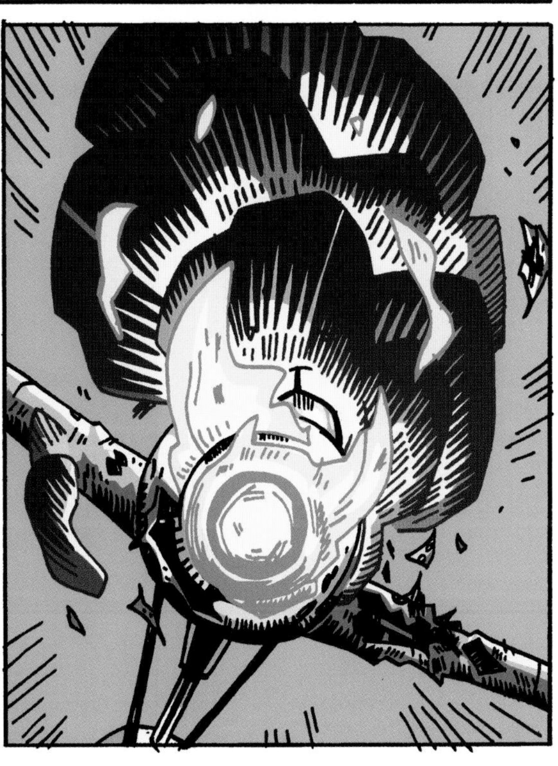

CAP?

KA-FOOM

M'FINE. GET BACK TO YER GUNS.

FEELS LIKE WE'RE DRAGGIN' A ***BOULDER*** PORTSIDE.
SMELLS LIKE BURNING.
LIZ. NEED YOU GO PUT OUT SOME FIRES BACK IN ENGINEERING. MAYBE LITERALLY.

ON IT, CAP.

WE WON'T MAKE IT, WILL WE.
SARA. FIRE UP THE RADIO. WE GOTTA GET SOME HELP.

YOU THINK WE HAVE FRIENDS?
NOT FRIENDS EXACTLY.

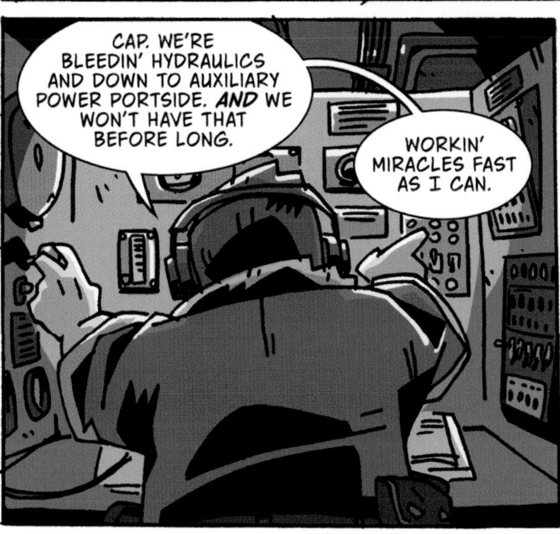
CAP. WE'RE BLEEDIN' HYDRAULICS AND DOWN TO AUXILIARY POWER PORTSIDE. AND WE WON'T HAVE THAT BEFORE LONG.
WORKIN' MIRACLES FAST AS I CAN.

CAP. SO LONG AS WE STILL GOT AN ANTENNA OUT THERE, YOU'RE ON AIR.

ANY A'YOU PIRATICAL PACIFIC BASTARDS CAN HEAR ME, LISTEN GOOD.
THIS HERE'S CAPTAIN CARTER OF THE SHE-DEVILS BROADCASTIN' FROM THE HARBINGER OF DOOM RECENTLY LIBERATED FROM MAD JACK.

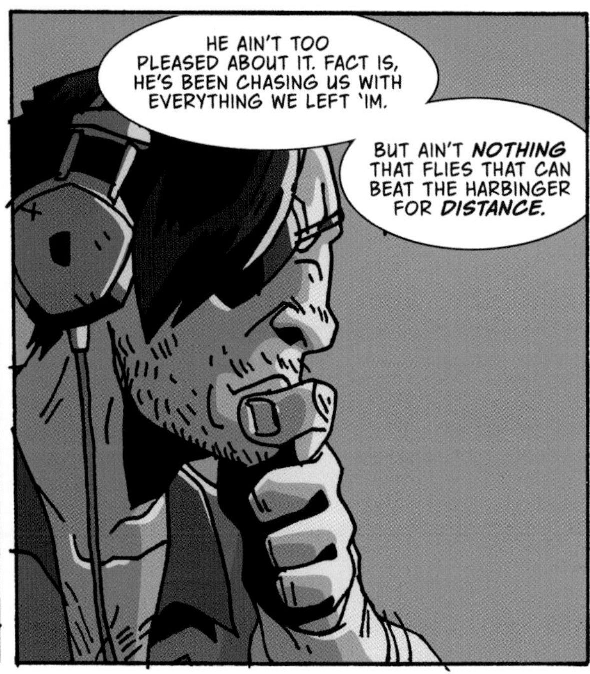
HE AIN'T TOO PLEASED ABOUT IT. FACT IS, HE'S BEEN CHASING US WITH EVERYTHING WE LEFT 'IM.
BUT AIN'T NOTHING THAT FLIES THAT CAN BEAT THE HARBINGER FOR DISTANCE.

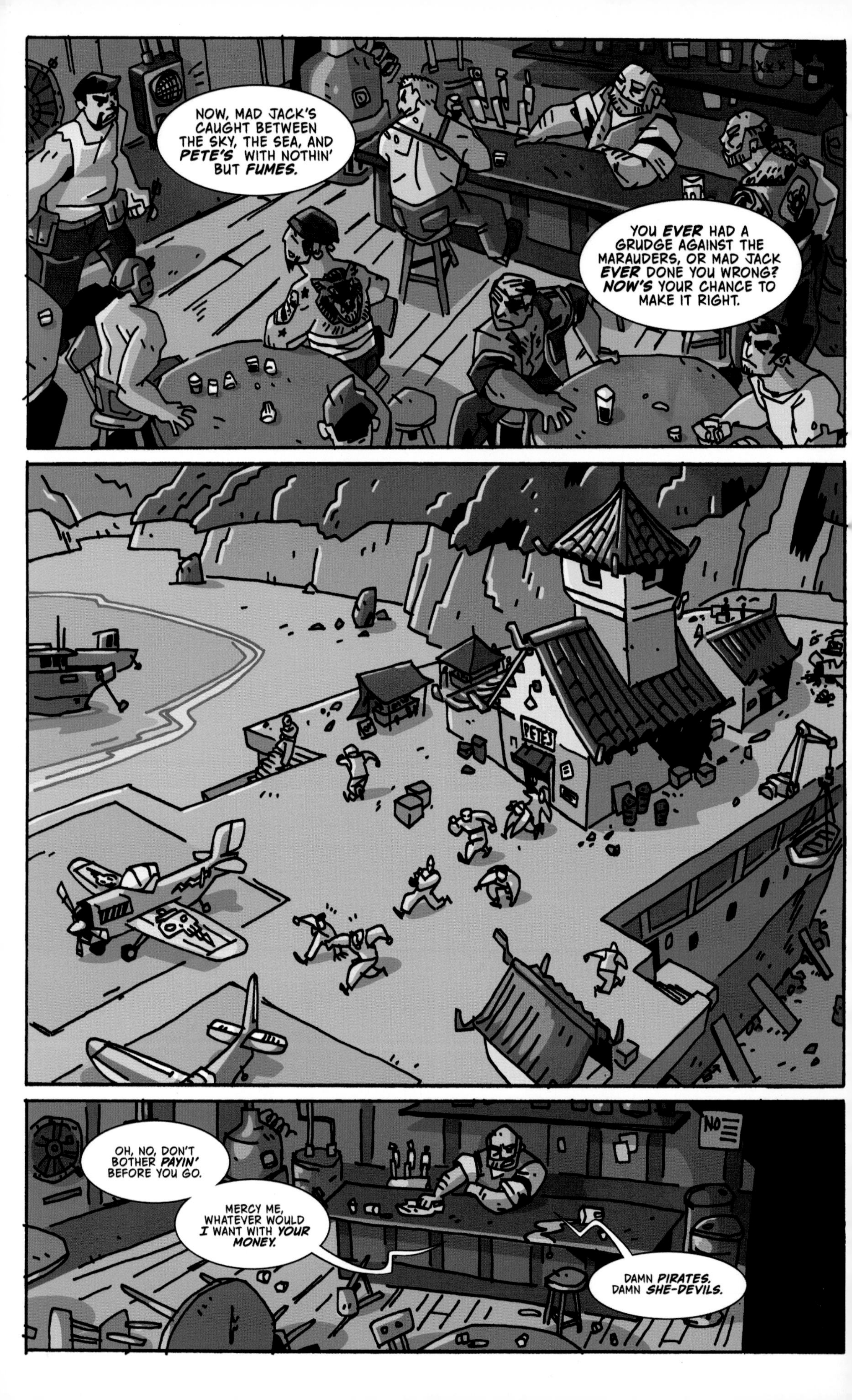
NOW, MAD JACK'S CAUGHT BETWEEN THE SKY, THE SEA, AND PETE'S WITH NOTHIN' BUT FUMES.
YOU EVER HAD A GRUDGE AGAINST THE MARAUDERS, OR MAD JACK EVER DONE YOU WRONG? NOW'S YOUR CHANCE TO MAKE IT RIGHT.
PETE'S
NO
OH, NO, DON'T BOTHER PAYIN' BEFORE YOU GO.
MERCY ME, WHATEVER WOULD I WANT WITH YOUR MONEY.
DAMN PIRATES. DAMN SHE-DEVILS.

ART BY SCOTT WEGENER
COLORS BY ANTHONY CLARK

EYE OF THE STORM

5

I REPEAT. MAD JACK AND HIS MARAUDERS ARE RUNNIN' ON FUMES AND PRAYERS. YOU WANT ANY OF 'EM DEAD, NOW'S YOUR CHANCE.
CLEAR THE CHANNEL! MAD JACK'S GOT ORDERS.
THEM SHE-DEVILS THINK THEY GOT THE BEST OF US.

BUT ALL THEY DONE IS SIGN THEIR OWN DEATH WARRANT.

IT'S GONNA BE A GOOD HOUR BEFORE THEIR CLEVER LITTLE TRICK PAYS OFF.
SHOW ME WHAT YOU MANIACS CAN DO IN AN HOUR!

CAP. I DONE ALL I *CAN* FOR THE PORTSIDE ENGINES AND HYDRAULICS WITHOUT *CLIMBIN'* OUT THERE.

LET'S HOPE IT DON'T COME TO THAT.
HOW WE DOIN' WITH THE BOGEYS, GIRLS?

NOTHING.
NO BOGEY.

CAP. CHATTER ON THE WIRELESS.
FAINT BUT *LOTS* OF IT. AND GETTIN' *STRONGER.* BEARING FROM PETE'S. I'D SAY YOUR TRICK PAID OFF.

ALL WE GOT TO DO NOW IS *LIVE* LONG ENOUGH FOR THAT TO *MATTER.*
EVERYONE. TAKE A GUN.

NO CAN DO, CAP. I GOTTA MASSAGE *EVERY* SYSTEM MINUTE BY MINUTE IF WE'RE TO GET ANYWHERE *NEAR* THE RENDEZVOUS.
ROGER. EVERYONE *ELSE*, TAKE A GUN. THAT MEANS YOU TOO, VAL.

KEEPING YOUR SHIRTS ON.

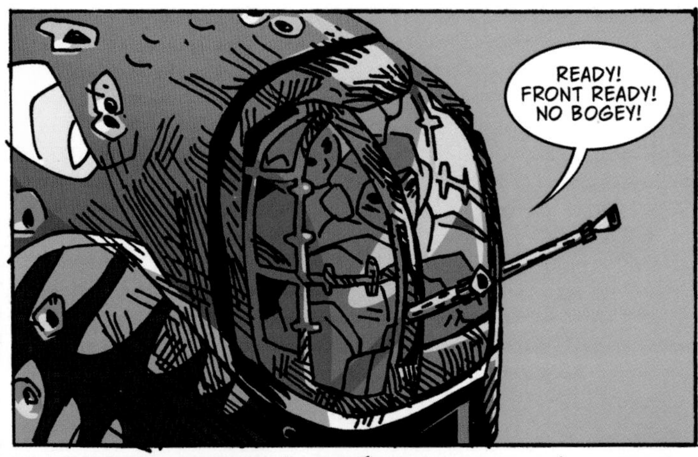
READY! FRONT READY! NO BOGEY!

TAKE GUN. STAY SAFE.

WE LEFT SAFE AT THE DOCK.

CAP? I CAN SEE 'EM.
MAD JACK'S COMIN'. THEY'RE *ALL* COMIN'.

YOU REMEMBER. *CHATTA, CHAT.*
YES!

CHATTA, CHAT!

TWOK
PAK
SRWANG
PAK
CHATTA
CHATTA

EVERYBODY HANG ON.
IF Y'CAN.

CAP. I DON'T MEAN TO HARP ON YER FLYIN', BUT MY JOB BACK HERE IS HARD ENOUGH WITHOUT YOU TAKIN' US OFF COURSE!

I GOT A PLAN. AND IT'S ONLY TAKIN' US A HAIR OFF COURSE.

SHE-DEVILS!
LOOK AT WHAT YOU DONE. LOOK WHAT YOU MADE US DO.
I TRIED REASONING WITH YOU. NO ONE CAN SAY DIFFERENT.
WE'RE DEAD WITHOUT THEM WOMEN.

WE GOT NOTHIN' TO LOSE NOW.

HOW 'BOUT YOU?

I GOT 'EM,
I GOT 'EM!

C'MON.

DEAD IN MY SIGHTS! DEAD, I TELL YA!

ZPWING!
TOK
AHH!
PWANG
TOK
TOK

CARTER!

CARTER!

MAY!

AHAHA! GOT 'EM, BOSS! DID YOU SEE! DID YOU SEE!
PAK
TOK

'FRAID THEY GOT YOU, VAL.

BLEEDING. ARE YOU HIT?
IT'S JUST THE GLASS.
FIND ME SOME GOGGLES TO KEEP THE WIND OUT MY GOOD EYE.

CAP. IF YOU'RE STILL ALIVE, WE *REALLY* NEED TO GET BACK ON COURSE.

ROGER THAT, LIZ. YOU WON'T LIKE IT THOUGH.
MAYBE. BUT I'LL HATE IT IF YOU *DON'T.*

YOU TOOK US OFF COURSE TO FLYING *INTO* THAT?

NOT GONNA LIE, VAL. WE DON'T HAVE A *CHANCE.*
BUT THAT STORM'S THE CLOSEST THING WE *GOT* TO ONE.

LOOK AT THEM RUN!
THEY FEAR OUR FURY MORE THAN THE STORM!
LET US SHOW THEM WHY!

PAK
TAK
TOK
WHATEVER THE PLAN IS, WE NEED A NEW ONE!
TAK
POK
TOK

LOST AN ENGINE!

CAP, IF WE DON'T DO SOMETHIN' SOON WE WON'T DO ANYTHING EVER AGAIN!
WORKIN' ON IT.

LIZ. GIVE THE REST OF THE ENGINES EVERYTHING THEY GOT!
AND THEN GIVE 'EM A LITTLE MORE.

DON'T LIKE THE LOOK OF THIS, CAP.
AIN'T DOIN' IT CAUSE IT'S PRETTY.

CAP, I DONE ALL I CAN WITH WHAT WE GOT. BUT WHAT WE GOT AIN'T MUCH.
TWO GOOD ENGINES, ONE ON ITS LAST LEG, AND ALL THREE RUNNIN' HOT ON A HOOCH THAT COULD BLOW ALL OF 'EM ANY SECOND.

LEMME FIX OUR POSITION WHILE WE STILL GOT SOME VISIBILITY. I'LL FEEL BETTER KNOWIN' WHERE WE DIED.

MEANWHILE, AT THE RENDEZVOUS...
I DON'T LIKE IT.

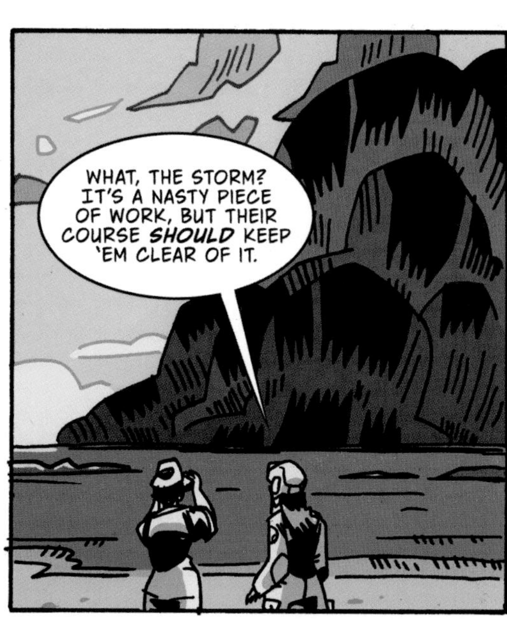
WHAT, THE STORM? IT'S A NASTY PIECE OF WORK, BUT THEIR COURSE SHOULD KEEP 'EM CLEAR OF IT.

YEAH, BUT WHAT IF THEY NEEDED TO CHANGE COURSE?

PLUS STORMS LIKE THAT TEAR UP SKY LIKE THEY GOT JETS STRAPPED TO 'EM. MIGHTA SWEPT UP OUR GALS BEFORE THEY KNEW WHAT HAPPENED.

ANYWAY, LAUREN, THANK YOU, BUT THERE'S NO SENSE WORRYING UNTIL THEY'RE LATE.

YOU'RE RIGHT, BUT THAT AIN'T STOPPIN' ME.

KRAKOOM
BOSS! WE LOST SIGHT OF 'EM!

OF COURSE Y'DID. THEY DIDN'T FLY INTO THIS TO MAKE IT EASY FOR US.
BUT IT'S WORSE FOR THEM. THEY'RE SCARED, THEY'RE HURT, AND THEY'RE OUTTA TRICKS.

JUST KEEP YOUR COURSE BEST YOU CAN AND DON'T HIT THE PLANE WHAT'S NEXT TO YA.

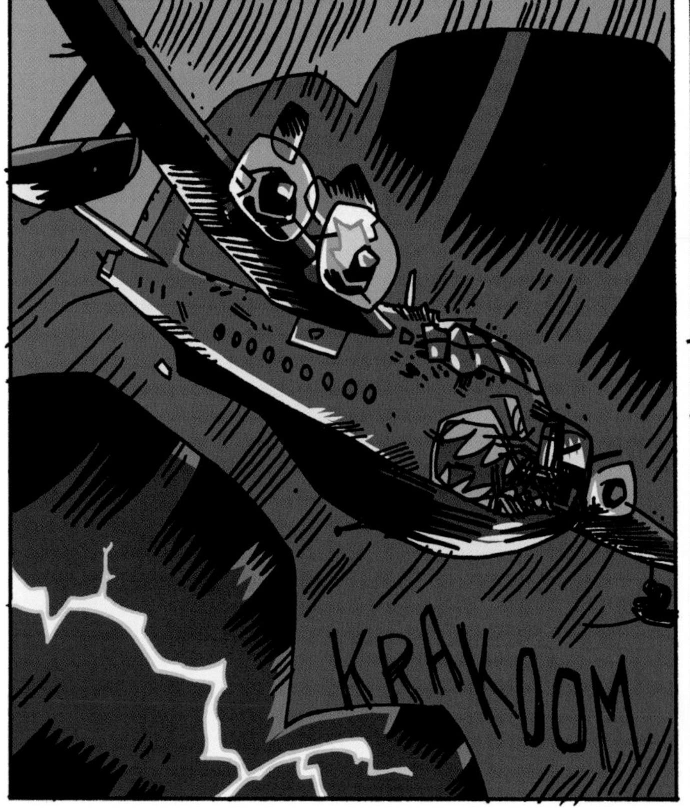
KRAKOOM

DON'T LIKE THE LOOK OF THAT LIGHTNING NEITHER.
IT'S THE LEAST DANGEROUS THING IN THE SKY RIGHT NOW.

INSTRUMENTS DEAD! STICK'S DEAD!

THERE IS FIRE WHERE ENGINE THERE WAS.

HALF OUR ELECTRONICS SHORTED OUT, CAP.
CAN YOU GET ME ENOUGH TO FLY WITH?

I'LL DIE TRYIN'.
SARA! MIND GIVIN' ME A HAND?

STILL HAVE WING. BUT MAYBE NOT FOR LONG.

THIS THING AIN'T GONNA ZAP ME, IS IT?
ONLY IF WE GET IT WORKIN'.

WE DONE IT!

EVEN THE *STORM* FEARS MAD JACK'S MARAUDERS!
BELAY THE CHATTER!

WE'RE TOSSED ALL OVER CREATION! BEAR UP ON MY POSITION!
AND KEEP AN EYE OUT FOR THEM SHE-DEVILS.

NO SIGN OF 'EM, BOSS! NOR IN THE SEA NOR SKY.
WHICH THE STORM'S WHAT GOT 'EM, IT DID.

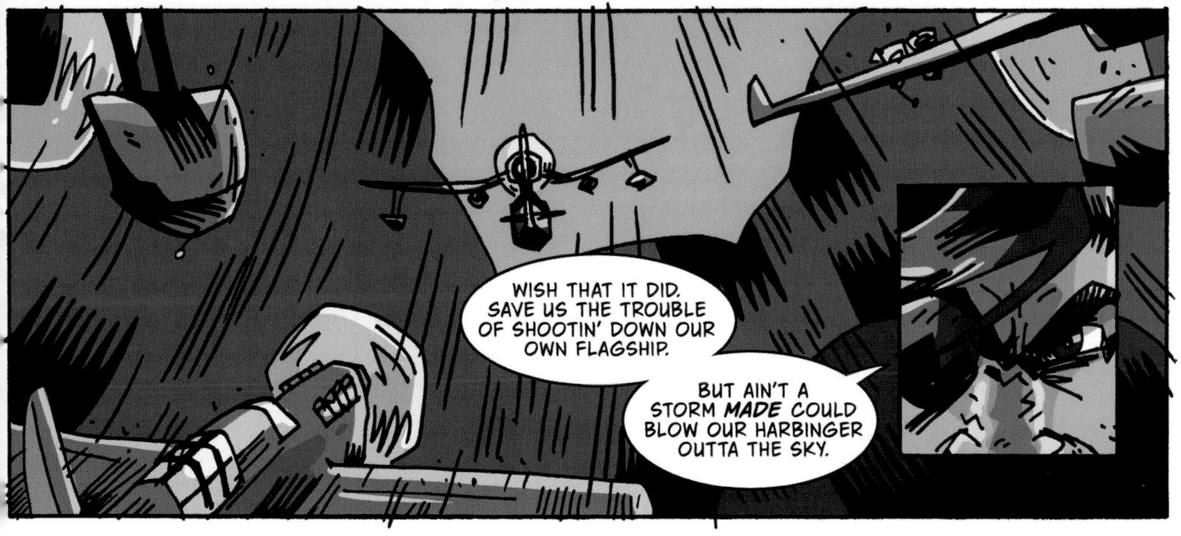
WISH THAT IT DID. SAVE US THE TROUBLE OF SHOOTIN' DOWN OUR OWN FLAGSHIP.
BUT AIN'T A STORM *MADE* COULD BLOW OUR HARBINGER OUTTA THE SKY.

VWOOM
SKRAKK
MARAUDERS!
RAMMING SPEED!
BWARRR
VOOM

ART BY SCOTT WEGENER
COLORS BY ANTHONY CLARK

NOTHING LEFT
BUT REVENGE
6

COME AROUND! THEY'RE FLYING FOR THEIR LIVES.

RIP 'EM FROM THE SKIES!

YOU HEARD THE BOSS!
BRING ABOUT EVERY GUN WE GOT!

THINK THE STORM WAS THE WORST OF IT?
NO. NOT EVEN CLOSE.

PIRATE, PIRATE!

PIRATES. *CHATTA.*
NOT CHATTA CHATTA CHATTA.

BRAKKA BAKKA

CAP, WE CAN'T TAKE MUCH MORE!

DOIN' WHAT I CAN, LIZ.

UH, CAP? WE GOT MORE INCOMIN'. FROM PETE'S, I THINK.
POK
TAK
TOK

ABOUT DAMN TIME.
WHAT IF THEY ATTACK US?
THAT'S EASY. WE'RE DEAD.

THEM'S THE MARAUDERS, BOYS! BURN EVERY LAST ONE OF 'EM.
WHAT ABOUT THE SHE-DEVILS?
DON'T SHOOT 'EM. UNLESS YOU GOTTA.

BOSS, WE GOT INCOMIN'!

AUGH!
KAK
TAKKA
TAKKA
KRAK
TOK

POK
TAK
DAKKA
AKKA
THEY GOT THE DROP ON US!
TAK
TOK
ON **YER** SIX! ON **MY** SIX!

TAK
PAK
TAK

LOOKS LIKE EVERYONE'S TOO BUSY KILLIN' EACH **OTHER** TO COME AFTER **US.**

HERE'S HOPIN' THEY KEEP AT IT THEN. COME ON BACK, SARA.
WE LOSING SPEED. **AND** ALTITUDE.

I'M ALREADY PULLIN' EVERY TRICK IN THE BOOK JUST TO KEEP THESE ENGINES **RUNNIN'.**
AND AIN'T **NONE** OF THEM DOIN' **GREAT** AT IT NEITHER.

CAN WE MAKE A WATER LANDING?

WE COME THIS FAR! CANNOT QUIT NOW!

IT'LL BE ROUGH, BUT WE CAN DO IT.
WE'LL LOSE THAT WING. IT'S HURT **BAD.**

BRAKKA DAKKA
ANY MARAUDERS LEFT, *HEAR* THIS!

IT WERE THEM *SHE-DEVILS* WHAT BROUGHT THIS PLAGUE UPON US.

THEY TOOK OUR PLANE, OUR WOMEN, OUR FUEL, *AND* OUR BROTHERS.

THEY LEFT US WITH NOTHIN'.

NOTHIN' BUT *REVENGE!*

SPUTTER
SPUF
PWEHHH

GOTTA SET 'ER DOWN, CAP. **FAST.**
BUT ALSO ***NICE*** AND ***EASY.***

WE GOT IT. ALMOST THERE.

BRAKKADAKKADAKKA

HANG ON!

SHRRRIPP

PLOOOSH

SHRANK

ARE WE STOPPED?
STOPPED FOR GOOD. THERE'S NO WINGS.

THEY COMING AROUND!
WE'RE SITTIN' DUCKS.

PIRATE!

CHATTA
CHATTA
CHATTA

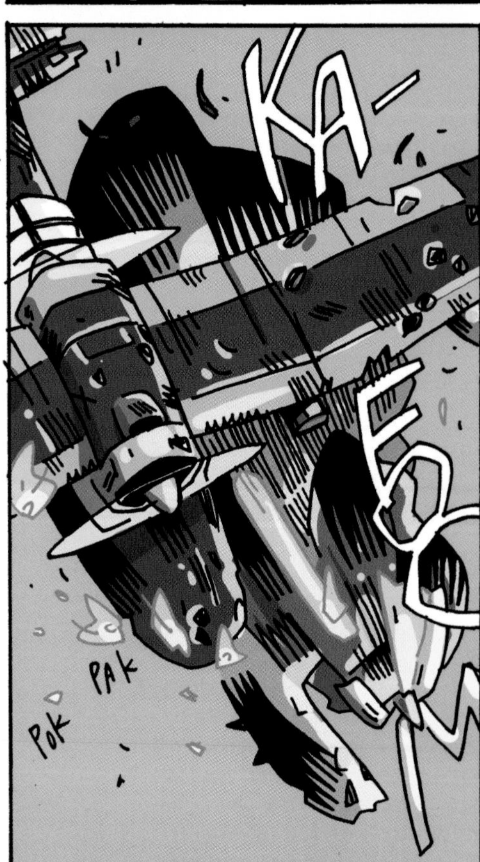
KA-
PAK
POK

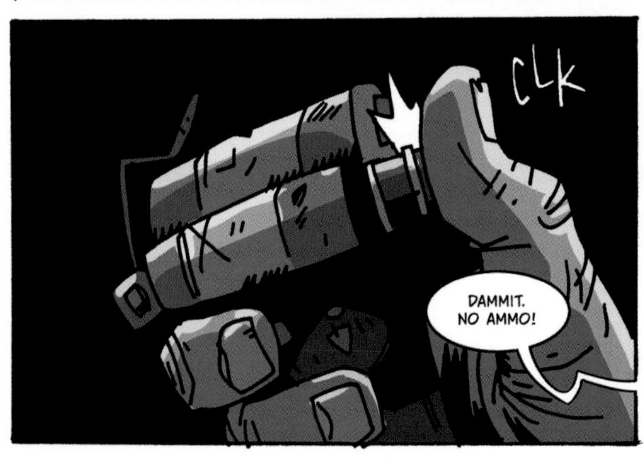
CLK
DAMMIT. NO AMMO!

DON'T NEED GUNS TO KILL YOU.

TNK
TNK

SEE THIS?

SPLK
YOU'RE DEAD.

SHROOOOSH

KRABOOOM

UH.

DIDN'T KNOW THIS WAS A *RECRUITMENT* DRIVE.

THEM? JUST ABOUT *NOTHING* WENT TO PLAN ON THIS RUN.

Y'DON'T SAY.
PLOOSH

TOLD YA IT'D WORK.
YEAH, FOR JUST ABOUT A WHOLE MINUTE.

THE PROBLEM ISN'T THE PACK. IT'S THE FUEL.
JUST GOTTA FIND THE RIGHT MIX. HOT ENOUGH TO JUST BARELY BE SAFE.
I'D SAY HAVIN' TROUBLE WITH THE FUEL IS WHAT'S WRONG WITH THE PACK.

YOU SHOULD HAVE A TALK WITH THE LADIES.

GUESS YOU'LL WANT YOUR HAT BACK.
I WASN'T GONNA **SAY** ANYTHING, BUT I WAS ***THINKIN'*** IT.

BWUHHH.

PIRATES!

CAP!

GRRAH!
D'AH!

MY PLANE! MY WOMEN!

PIRATES!

I GOTCHA.

CUT THE ENGINES!
GIRLS OVERBOARD!

THE END.

THE SPARROW

IN PROJECT MILLIPEDE

PAS-DE-CALAIS, FRANCE
MAY, 1944
SUPPOSED TO BE A FARMHOUSE.
BLOODY USELESS.
!

ONE WEEK EARLIER...
AH, SPARROW. DO COME IN.

DRINK?
PLEASE.

WHAT WILL YOU HAVE?
WHATEVER YOU'RE POURING IS MARVELOUS, I'M SURE.

I'LL COME STRAIGHT TO IT.
OUR AGENTS WITHIN THE FRENCH RESISTANCE HAVE UNCOVERED THE JERRIES' NEWEST "WONDER WEAPON." YOU WILL SABOTAGE IT.

WILL THERE BE AMERICAN INTERFERENCE?
NOT THIS TIME. NO, I DON'T BELIEVE THE YANKS ARE EVEN AWARE OF THIS PROJECT.

IT IS UNIQUELY DANGEROUS TO BRITISH INTERESTS.

<GET HER HANDS.>
BLAM
AUUGH!
HRK
KCHK
KCHK

IS THIS TO BE *BELIEVED?*
SIX *HUNDRED* ARTILLERY ROUNDS PER *HOUR?*
IT IS.

AIMED *DIRECTLY* AT LONDON.

THE *V-3* CANNON. CODENAMED "MILLIPEDE." A MULTI-CHAMBERED, MULTI-BARRELED ARTILLERY SYSTEM.
AND COMPLETELY SUBTERRANEAN.
NOTHING TO BOMB BUT THE TERMINUS OF THE GUN BARRELS THEMSELVES.
AND *THOSE* ARE TOO SMALL TO SCORE A HIT. NAZI BASTARDS.

YOU'LL HAVE TO INFILTRATE THE FACILITY. INTELLIGENCE SUGGESTS THE SEA-SIDE CLIFF IS YOUR BEST CHANCE, SO YOU'LL BE *MINIMALLY* EQUIPPED, I'M AFRAID.
DON'T WORRY. OUR FROGGY FRIENDS ASSURE ME THERE WILL BE A SUPPLY DROP AT A NEARBY FARMHOUSE. EXPLOSIVES MOSTLY.

SABOTAGE THE CANNONS AND EXFILTRATE.

BLAM BLAM BLAM
BLAM BLAM

BLAM!
!
!

<COME OUT!>

<WE HAVE YOU SURROUNDED!>
THAT A FACT, FRITZ?

<SLOWLY!>
<LITTLE HELP? HE'S IN THE WAY.>

BLAM
BLAM
WHY THE **HELL** WOULD YOU THINK I ONLY BROUGHT **ONE** GUN?

V-3 COMMAND CENTER
<SIR. RECON SQUAD WOLF HAS YET TO CHECK IN.>

<ESTABLISH CONTACT.>

<EAGLE TO WOLF. RESPOND.>

EAGLE TO WOLF. RESPOND IMMEDIATELY.>

<NOTHING, SIR.>
<THEY'VE SENT THE SPARROW.>

<THIS IS COMMANDER SCHNEIDER. AN ENEMY AGENT HAS BREACHED THE PERIMETER.>
<SECURITY TEAMS ARE TO CONDUCT A FULL SEARCH OF THE GROUNDS. THE ENTIRE FACILITY IS ON HIGH ALERT UNTIL FURTHER NOTICE.>

TSK.
THEY'RE DETERMINED TO MAKE THIS DIFFICULT.
NO BACKUP.
FICTIONAL SUPPLY DROP.
AND AN AMBUSH FIRST THING.
BLOODY MISSION WAS COMPROMISED BEFORE I EVER SET OFF.

tung
tung

klung
!
<YOU HEAR THAT?>
<SOUNDS LIKE ***SQUIRRELS*** IN THE GUN AGAIN.>

<A SQUIRREL THE SIZE OF A ***HORSE,*** THEN.>
<YOU CAN'T FIT A ***HORSE*** IN THERE.>
KTONG

BWANG

D'OOF!

<THERE MUST BE AN UPDATE.>
<NOTHING, SIR.>

<SIR. WE FOUND WOLF SQUAD.>
<GIVE ME THE RADIO.>

<ALL DEAD, SIR.>
<AND PICKED OVER.>

<PERIMETER PATROLS HAVE FOUND NOTHING ELSE?>
<NOTHING, SIR. ALL CHECKPOINTS INTO THE STATION ARE SECURE.>
<SHE MAY BE HIDING. WAITING FOR US TO LOWER OUR GUARD.>

SHE COULD BE ANYWHERE...

<NO. IT'S THE *CANNONS.*>
<SIR?>
<DIVERT ALL SEARCH TEAMS. LOCK DOWN THE CANNON ACCESS TUNNELS AND CONDUCT A FULL SWEEP. EACH ONE.>

<WE WILL FLUSH HER OUT.>

!
HMM.

FWHAMF
WHAM
KLUD
AUGH!
KRKT
<CANNON FIVE! TUNNEL ONE!>
KRNCH

KCHK

<SHE'S HEADING STRAIGHT FOR THE AMBUSH.>

<HITLER'S ORDERS ARE TO KILL ENEMY COMMANDOS.>

ONE HOUR LATER

<CAN'T HELP BUT NOTICE I'M STILL BREATHING.>
<YOU ARE.>
<DO YOU BREAK YOUR FUEHRER'S ORDERS OFTEN?>

<OH, YOU MUSTN'T THINK OF THIS AS ANY KIND OF REPRIEVE. NO, YOU WILL DIE. IN THIS ROOM, MOST LIKELY.>
<BUT FIRST YOU WILL TELL US EVERYTHING YOU KNOW.>

<OH, YES? GOOD LUCK.>
<I HAVE NO DOUBT YOU WILL RESIST INTERROGATION TO THE UTMOST OF YOUR ABILITIES. AND WHILE THEY ARE CONSIDERABLE, THEY HAVE A LIMIT.>

<DON'T YOU GET IT, FRITZ? ALL THEY TELL ME IS THERE'S A NAZI BASTARD NEEDS KILLING AND WHERE TO FIND HIM.>
<I DON'T EVEN KNOW WHERE THE INTELLIGENCE COMES FROM.>

<OF COURSE THAT'S YOUR STORY.>
<YOU **KNOW** THERE IS NO ESCAPE, SO YOU'D PREFER TO **DIE** BEFORE WE EXTRACT ANY INFORMATION THAT MIGHT HINDER CHURCHILL'S EFFORTS.>

<SO YOU DON'T BELIEVE ME?>
<OF COURSE NOT.>
<THEN WHY WOULD YOU BELIEVE **ANYTHING** YOU GET OUT OF ME?>

<TO BE HONEST? THE INTELLIGENCE IS IRRELEVANT.>
<OUR TRUE AIM IS TO ALLOW YOUR COMRADES TO "DISCOVER" MY REPORT DETAILING **HOW** WE ACQUIRED IT.>

<WE'LL HAVE TO INCLUDE PICTURES OF WHAT REMAINS TO BE SURE THE POINT IS MADE.>

<THAT IS NOTHING TO SMILE ABOUT.>
<OH, IT'S NOT THAT.>
<YOU'VE GOT A GREAT PLAN. IT'S VERY CLEVER BUT IT'LL NEVER WORK.>
<NO? DO TELL. BY ALL MEANS.>
<IN ALL THE EXCITEMENT OF CAPTURING "THE SPARROW", YOU'VE OVERLOOKED SOMETHING.>
<YOUR SOLDIERS MUST'VE REPORTED ON IT. REMEMBER ALL THE ONES I LEFT FOR YOU?>
<HOW THEY'D BEEN STRIPPED OF WEAPONS AND AMMUNITION?>
<YOU MAY RECALL I DIDN'T HAVE ANY OF IT WHEN YOU CAPTURED ME.>
<I WONDER WHERE IT ALL WENT.>

<THE HELL ARE THOSE DOING OUT?>
<I DON'T KNOW HOW, BUT THIS IS HUFFMANN'S FAULT.>

<ARE YOU ALL RIGHT?>

BAFOOOOM
rrrmbl
<GOSH. I HOPE THERE ISN'T *MORE.*>
<SECURE THE PRISONER.>

WOULD YOU TWO STAND CLOSER TOGETHER, PLEASE?
<WHAT'D SHE SAY?>
<HOW SHOULD I KNOW?>
THANK YOU.
KRAKT

<FIRES NOW IN CANNONS THREE ***AND*** FOUR, SIR!>
<AND THE BLAST DOORS?>
<UNRESPONSIVE.>

<DISPATCH FIRE RESPONSE TEAMS TO ***EVERY*** POWDER ROOM. WE CAN'T RISK AN EXPLOSIVE CASCADE THROUGH THE ***ENTIRE*** FACILITY.>
<AND TURN ***OFF*** THE DAMN ***ALARMS!***>

KONK
?

KAFOOOOM

KTHROOOOOOM!
rmmmbl

<STATUS REPORT! WHERE ARE THE DAMNED FIRE RESPONSE TEAMS!>

KOFF
GOT TO BE A BETTER WAY TO DESTROY THIS BLOODY PLACE.

<LATEST CASUALTY REPORT, SIR. FIVE PERCENT DEAD, TWENTY PERCENT INJURED, AND ANOTHER TEN PERCENT UNACCOUNTED FOR.>
<CANNONS TWO, THREE, AND FOUR ARE INOPERABLE UNTIL THEIR PRIMARY FIRING CHAMBERS CAN BE REPLACED.>

<THAT CAN BE DONE IN A MATTER OF DAYS. WE CAN STILL ATTACK LONDON AND CRIPPLE THE ALLIED INVASION BEFORE IT BEGINS.>
<YES, SIR.>

<ARE THE FIRES EXTINGUISHED?>
<NO, SIR. BUT THEY ARE CONTAINED. MOSTLY.>

<MOSTLY CONTAINED IS NOT CONTAINED.>
<IT'S THE BEST WE CAN DO WITH OUR REDUCED MANPOWER.>

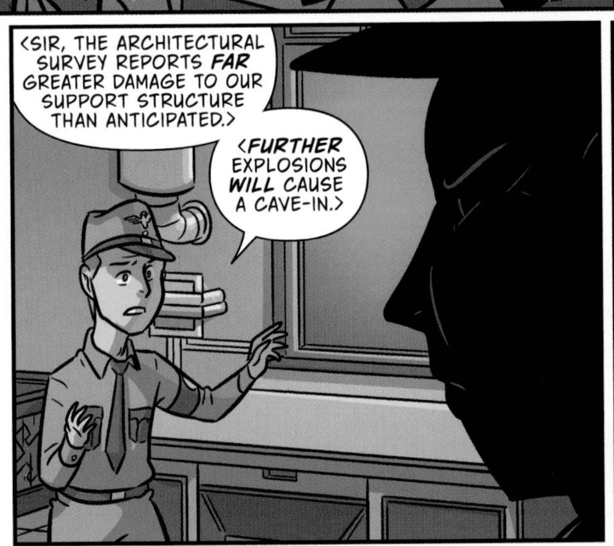
<SIR, THE ARCHITECTURAL SURVEY REPORTS FAR GREATER DAMAGE TO OUR SUPPORT STRUCTURE THAN ANTICIPATED.>
<FURTHER EXPLOSIONS WILL CAUSE A CAVE-IN.>

<IF WE CANNOT PUT OUT THEN FIRES, THEN WE WILL MOVE THE EXPLOSIVES.>
<TRANSPORT THE REMAINING CHARGES TO DEEP STORAGE.>

<THIS IS THE LAST BATCH, RIGHT?>
<IT IS, THANK GOD.>
<WE GET ALL THE FUN JOBS.>
<COULD BE WORSE.>
<HOW?>
<DUNNO. BUT THEY'LL *FIND* A WAY.>
TUNK
KTNK

DING
RUMMMMMMBLE
<SHE ESCAPED.>

<I DON'T KNOW **HOW** SHE DID IT...>
<COMMANDER! ***COMMANDER REINHOLD, SIR!***>

<SIR! WE ***MUST*** EVACUATE!>

<SIR!>

<THIS WAY. DO NOT USE THE ELEVATORS.>
<I'LL BE RIGHT BEHIND YOU.>

<IS ANYONE THERE!>

YES.

FWAM
KOFF

KAFOOOM
SECONDARY EXPLOSIONS.
GOOD.

UNLESS THEY COME THIS WAY.

BKOW

AUGH!
DO YOU KNOW THAT YOU'VE ACCOMPLISHED NOTHING?
YOU WERE MEANT TO DISCOVER THE V-3 FACILITY. SO THAT YOU WOULD COME HERE. SO THAT YOU WOULD ATTEMPT TO DESTROY IT.

DID A BIT BETTER THAN ATTEMPT, FRITZ.
HEH. OW.
FWUMP
AUGH!
DID IT NOT OCCUR TO YOU THAT THIS WOULD BE AN ACCEPTABLE LOSS?
YES, YOU DID EXCELLENT WORK HERE. YOU SINGLEHANDEDLY DEMOLISHED OUR V-3 WEAPON SYSTEM.
OUR WONDER WEAPONS WILL REDUCE LONDON TO ASHES. AND THEN MOSCOW AND THEN WASHINGTON.
YOU CHANGED NOTHING. YOU WILL DIE FOR NOTHING.

YOU--
SHOULD BE
BLEEDING?
BKAM

LATEST FROM Q BRANCH. BULLETPROOF JACKET.

STILL HURTS LIKE HELL THOUGH.

PUMF
HHHHRK

BUT NOT AS MUCH AS YOU'RE HURTING.

NAZI BASTARD.
PAIN AND DEATH IS ALL YOU DESERVE.

BKAM
BKAM
BKAM

KRRRRAKT
KRK-BOOOM

BLOODY HELL!

WESTMINSTER
ONE MONTH LATER
THIS IS A TREASURE TROVE! THERE WERE YET *MORE* FILES, YOU SAY?
HUNDREDS. I GATHERED WHAT I COULD. ONLY WISH I'D HAVE FOUND *SOMETHING* ON THE V-4 *OR* V-5.
WE KNOW THEY *EXIST.* IT'S A START.
IT'S NOT ENOUGH.
YOU WERE SURROUNDED BY *FIRE* AND *NAZIS,* SPARROW. FRANKLY, THAT YOU MADE IT OUT *ALIVE* IS MIRACLE ENOUGH.
WHICH RATHER BRINGS ME TO A *LARGER* POINT.

WHEN THE *PREVIOUS* SPARROW DIED--
MY BROTHER WAS *KILLED.*

--ER, YES, OF COURSE. WHEN HE WAS *KILLED,* WHITEHALL WAS RATHER AT A LOSS. IT WAS A BLOW TO THE ENTIRE FOREIGN INTELLIGENCE OFFICE.
BUT THEN YOU TOOK UP THE MANTLE.

THERE MUST ALWAYS BE A SPARROW, SIR.
QUITE RIGHT. BUT WHITEHALL BELIEVES IT'S TIME FOR THE SPARROW TO CHANGE.

I HAVE NEVER BALKED AT AN ORDER, AND WHILE I WILL NOT BOAST, I WILL POINT OUT THAT MY RECORD IS WITHOUT REPROACH.
SPARROW.

AND IN ANY CASE, THE SPARROW IS A LINEAGE, AND AS I'M THE LAST, I SHOULD LIKE TO SEE HOW WHITEHALL THINKS--

SPARROW!
YOU'RE NOT BEING REPLACED. YOU'RE BEING PROMOTED.

PROMOTED?

QUITE. TO MILITARY INTELLIGENCE SECTION 18.
THE--BUT THERE IS NO SECTION 18.

AS OF THIS MORNING, THERE RATHER IS.
CONGRATULATIONS, DIRECTOR.

AN EXPANSION OF THE SPARROW'S ROLE, YOU SEE.
YOU WILL COORDINATE INFILTRATION, ESPIONAGE, AND ASSASSINATION MISSIONS ACROSS AN ELITE TEAM OF THE ALLIES' BEST AGENTS.
AND ATOMIC ROBO.
HE'S BULLETPROOF. WE CAN FIND A WAY TO USE HIM.
WE WON'T HAVE TO USE HIM MUCH.
I'LL DRINK TO THAT.
THE END

FROM TESLADYNE LABS

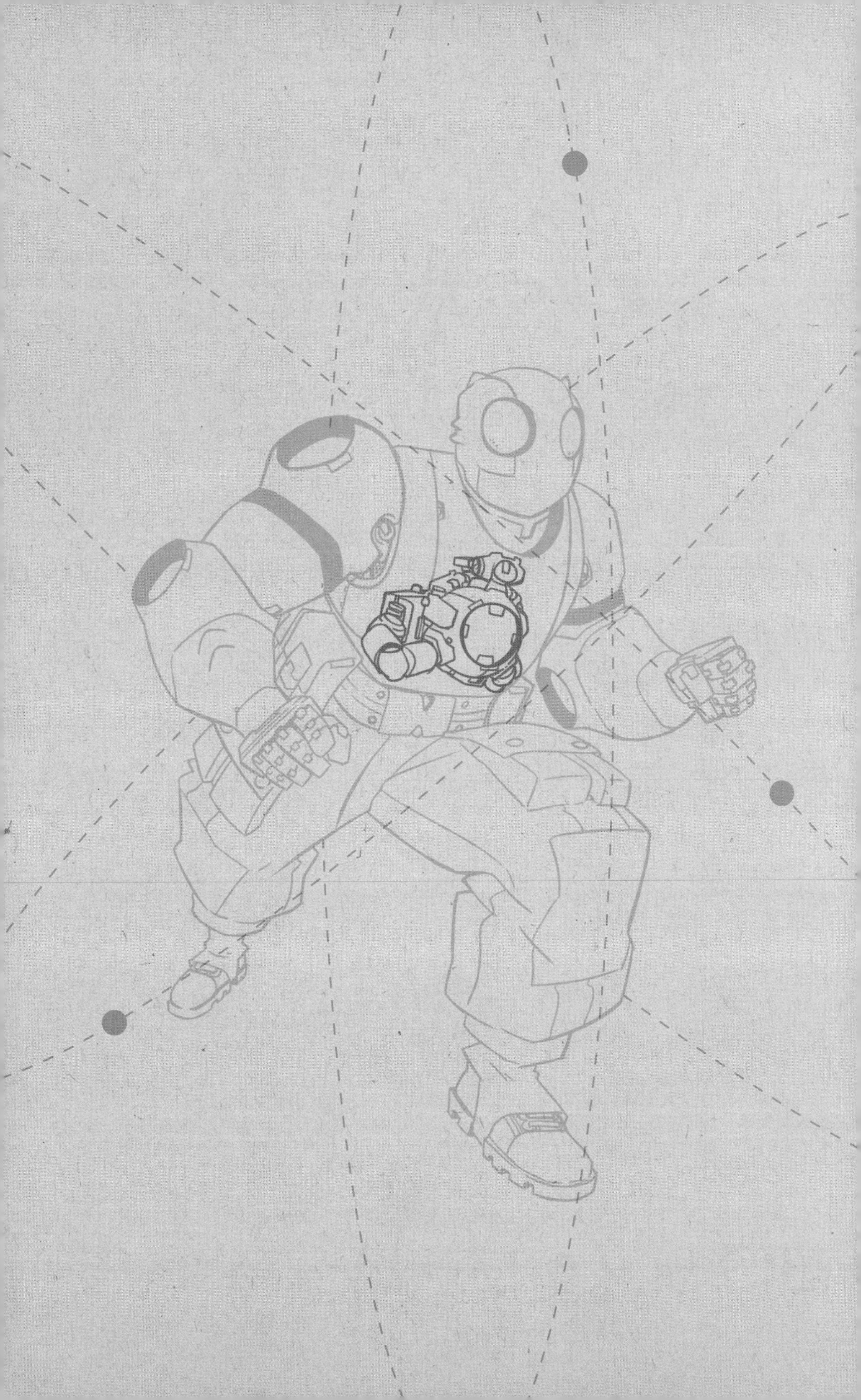

AFTERWORD

IT'S NO SECRET THE FLYING SHE-DEVILS ARE MY FAVORITE part of Atomic Robo's world. We wanted to tell their story as soon as we finished our first series but it took us years to work up the courage and the skill to pull it off. When it came time to expand Robo's world through *Real Science Adventures* I knew what we had to do and I sat down to make an airtight case for it. Here it is in full:

BRIAN MORE SHE-DEVILS NOW NOW

It worked like a charm.

Scott Wegener
RVA

THROUGH THE FLYING SHE-DEVILS WE'RE ABLE TO TRANSFORM one third of the surface of the Earth into a badlands filled with mercenaries, pirates (both air and sea varieties), warlords, and hidden sci-fi enclaves. We started with their final adventure in the pages of *Atomic Robo*, so it seemed only fitting to go back to something from their early days with *Real Science Adventures*.

Next I guess we've got to fill in the stuff that happens in between!

Brian Clevinger
RVA

"DRAWING PLANES CAN'T BE TOO HARD, RIGHT?" Famous last words. I was given an opportunity to draw a She-Devils book, and wasn't going to let a little thing like not knowing how to draw airplanes get in the way of such sheer awesomeness. Turns out that drawing planes is, in fact, freakin' hard. Who knew?

What I really wasn't expecting over the course of my research, though, was to fall in love with these marvels of engineering, and the brave, clever folk of all countries who flew them during WW2. From wingspans to loadouts, every plane tells a story to me now. And sometimes, like with Short Sunderlands, they just happen to tell stories about kick-ass ladies shooting pirates out of the Polynesian sky.

Lo Baker
http://aquapunk.co/

SPARROW IS SUCH AN EASY CHARACTER TO DRAW FOR. I love drawing action and add on that she's kicking Nazi butt made doing this comic that much more fun! Haha I wish I could be her sidekick! As a fan I can't wait to read what happens next for her and I hope I get a chance to draw Sparrow again someday!

Wook Jin Clark
http://wookjinclark.com/